WHERE'S WALDO?

THE ULTIMATE TRAVEL COLLECTION

MARTIN HANDFORD

CANDLEWICK PRESS

HI, WALDO-WATCHER!

ARE YOU READY TO JOIN ME ON MY FIVE FANTASTIC ADVENTURES?

WHERE'S WALDO?
WHERE'S WALDO NOW?
WHERE'S WALDO? THE FANTASTIC JOURNEY
WHERE'S WALDO? IN HOLLYWOOD
WHERE'S WALDO? THE WONDER BOOK

CAN YOU FIND THE FIVE INTREPID TRAVELERS AND THEIR PRECIOUS ITEMS IN EVERY SCENE?

ODLAW   WIZARD   WENDA   WOOF   WALDO
         WHITEBEARD

 WALDO'S KEY   WOOF'S BONE   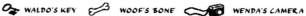 WENDA'S CAMERA

 WIZARD WHITEBEARD'S SCROLL   ODLAW'S BINOCULARS

WAIT, THERE'S MORE! AT THE BEGINNING AND END OF EACH ADVENTURE, FIND A FOLD-OUT CHECKLIST WITH HUNDREDS MORE THINGS TO LOOK FOR.

WOW! WHAT A SEARCH!

BON VOYAGE!

Waldo

ON THE BEACH

WHERE'S WALDO?

HI, FRIENDS!

MY NAME IS WALDO. I'M JUST SETTING OFF ON A WORLDWIDE HIKE. YOU CAN COME TOO. ALL YOU HAVE TO DO IS FIND ME.

I'VE GOT ALL I NEED — WALKING STICK, KETTLE, MALLET, CUP, BACKPACK, SLEEPING BAG, BINOCULARS, CAMERA, SNORKEL, BELT, BAG, AND SHOVEL.

BY THE WAY, I'M NOT TRAVELING ON MY OWN. WHEREVER I GO, THERE ARE LOTS OF OTHER CHARACTERS FOR YOU TO SPOT. FIRST FIND WOOF (BUT ALL YOU CAN SEE IS HIS TAIL), WENDA, WIZARD WHITEBEARD, AND ODLAW. THERE ARE ALSO 25 WALDO-WATCHERS SOMEWHERE, EACH OF WHOM APPEARS ONLY ONCE IN MY TRAVELS. CAN YOU FIND ONE OTHER CHARACTER WHO APPEARS IN EVERY SCENE? ALSO IN EVERY SCENE, CAN YOU SPOT WIZARD WHITEBEARD'S SCROLL, MY KEY, WOOF'S BONE, WENDA'S CAMERA, AND ODLAW'S BINOCULARS?

WOW! WHAT A SEARCH! Waldo

THE GREAT WHERE'S WALDO? CHECKLIST: PART ONE

Hundreds of things for Waldo-Watchers to watch out for! Don't forget PART TWO at the end of this adventure!

IN TOWN

- [ ] A dog on a roof
- [ ] A man on a fountain
- [ ] A man about to trip over a dog's leash
- [ ] A car crash
- [ ] A happy barber
- [ ] People on a street, watching TV
- [ ] A puncture caused by a Roman arrow
- [ ] A tearful tune
- [ ] A boy attacked by a plant
- [ ] A waiter who isn't concentrating
- [ ] A robber who's been clobbered
- [ ] A face on a wall
- [ ] A man coming out of a manhole
- [ ] A man feeding pigeons
- [ ] A bicycle crash

ON THE BEACH

- [ ] A dog biting a boy's bottom
- [ ] A man who is overdressed
- [ ] A muscular man with a medal
- [ ] A popular girl
- [ ] A water-skier on water
- [ ] A striped photo
- [ ] A punctured air mattress
- [ ] A donkey who likes ice cream
- [ ] A man being squashed
- [ ] A punctured beach ball
- [ ] A human pyramid
- [ ] A human stepping-stone
- [ ] Two odd friends
- [ ] A cowboy
- [ ] A human donkey
- [ ] Age and beauty
- [ ] A boy who follows in his father's footsteps
- [ ] Two men with vests, one without
- [ ] A boy being tortured by a spider
- [ ] A show-off with sand castles
- [ ] A gang of hat robbers
- [ ] An Arab making pyramids
- [ ] Three protruding tongues
- [ ] Two oddly fitting hats
- [ ] An odd couple
- [ ] Five spiders
- [ ] A towel with a hole in it
- [ ] A punctured pontoon boat
- [ ] A boy who's not allowed any ice cream

SKI SLOPES

- [ ] A man reading on a roof
- [ ] A flying skier
- [ ] A runaway skier
- [ ] A backward skier
- [ ] A portrait in snow
- [ ] An illegal fisherman
- [ ] A snowball in the neck
- [ ] Two unconscious skiers
- [ ] Two skiers hitting trees
- [ ] An Alpine horn
- [ ] A snow skier
- [ ] A flag collector
- [ ] Two very scruffy skiers
- [ ] A skier up a tree
- [ ] A water-skier on snow
- [ ] An abominable snowman
- [ ] A skiing reindeer
- [ ] A roof jumper
- [ ] A heap of skaters

CAMPSITE

- [ ] A bull in a hedge
- [ ] Bull horns
- [ ] A shark in a canal
- [ ] A bull seeing red
- [ ] A careless kick
- [ ] Tea in a lap
- [ ] A low bridge
- [ ] People knocked over by a mallet
- [ ] A man surprised undressing
- [ ] A bicycle tire about to be punctured
- [ ] Camper's camels
- [ ] A scarecrow that doesn't work
- [ ] A wigwam
- [ ] Large biceps
- [ ] A collapsed tent
- [ ] A smoking barbecue
- [ ] A fisherman catching old boots
- [ ] An old-fashioned bicycle
- [ ] Boy Scouts making fire
- [ ] A roller-skating hiker
- [ ] A man blowing up a boat
- [ ] A camper's butler
- [ ] Runners on a road
- [ ] A bull chasing children
- [ ] Scruffy campers
- [ ] Thirsty walkers

THE TRAIN STATION

- [ ] A boy falling from a train
- [ ] A breakdown on tracks
- [ ] Naughty children on a train roof
- [ ] People being knocked over by a door
- [ ] A man about to step on a ball
- [ ] Three different times at the same time
- [ ] A wheelbarrow baby carriage
- [ ] A face on a train
- [ ] Five people reading one newspaper
- [ ] A struggling bag carrier
- [ ] A show-off with suitcases
- [ ] A man losing everything from his cases
- [ ] A smoking train
- [ ] A squeeze on a bench
- [ ] A dog tearing a man's trousers
- [ ] Fare dodgers
- [ ] A hand caught between doors
- [ ] A cattle stampede
- [ ] A man breaking a weighing machine

AIRPORT

- [ ] A flying saucer
- [ ] A boy who's been hiding in a suitcase
- [ ] A child firing a catapult
- [ ] A leaking fuel pipe
- [ ] Flight controllers playing badminton
- [ ] A rocket
- [ ] A turret
- [ ] Three watch smugglers
- [ ] Naughty children on a plane
- [ ] A forklift truck
- [ ] A wind sock
- [ ] A chopper
- [ ] A plane that doesn't fly
- [ ] A flying Ace
- [ ] Dracula
- [ ] Five men blowing up a balloon
- [ ] Runners on a runway
- [ ] Four smoking people
- [ ] Four people falling from a plane
- [ ] A cargo of cattle
- [ ] A fire engine
- [ ] Three childish pilots
- [ ] A blimp being punctured

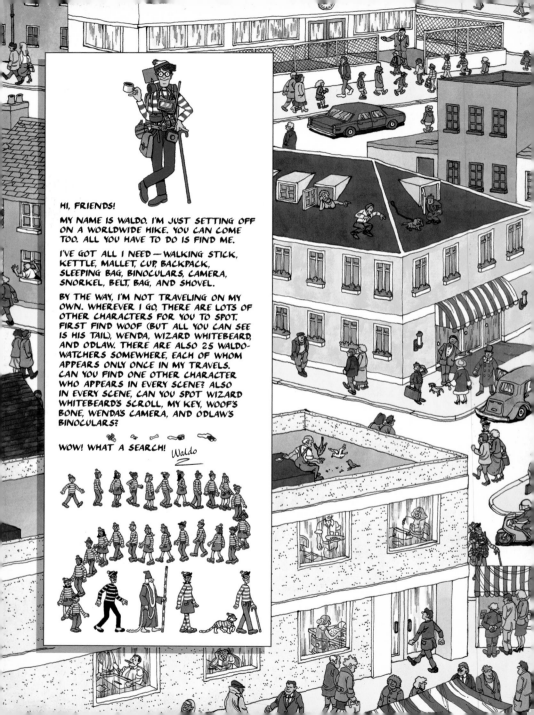

HI, FRIENDS!

MY NAME IS WALDO. I'M JUST SETTING OFF ON A WORLDWIDE HIKE. YOU CAN COME TOO. ALL YOU HAVE TO DO IS FIND ME.

I'VE GOT ALL I NEED — WALKING STICK, KETTLE, MALLET, CUP, BACKPACK, SLEEPING BAG, BINOCULARS, CAMERA, SNORKEL, BELT, BAG, AND SHOVEL.

BY THE WAY, I'M NOT TRAVELING ON MY OWN. WHEREVER I GO, THERE ARE LOTS OF OTHER CHARACTERS FOR YOU TO SPOT. FIRST FIND WOOF (BUT ALL YOU CAN SEE IS HIS TAIL), WENDA, WIZARD WHITEBEARD, AND ODLAW. THERE ARE ALSO 25 WALDO-WATCHERS SOMEWHERE, EACH OF WHOM APPEARS ONLY ONCE IN MY TRAVELS. CAN YOU FIND ONE OTHER CHARACTER WHO APPEARS IN EVERY SCENE? ALSO IN EVERY SCENE, CAN YOU SPOT WIZARD WHITEBEARD'S SCROLL, MY KEY, WOOF'S BONE, WENDA'S CAMERA, AND ODLAW'S BINOCULARS?

WOW! WHAT A SEARCH! Waldo

GREETINGS,
WALDO-FOLLOWERS!
WOW, THE BEACH WAS
GREAT TODAY! I SAW
THIS GIRL STICK AN
ICE-CREAM CONE IN HER
BROTHER'S FACE, AND
THERE WAS A SAND-
CASTLE WITH A REAL
KNIGHT IN ARMOR
INSIDE! FANTASTIC!

Waldo

TO:
WALDO-FOLLOWERS
HERE, THERE,
EVERYWHERE

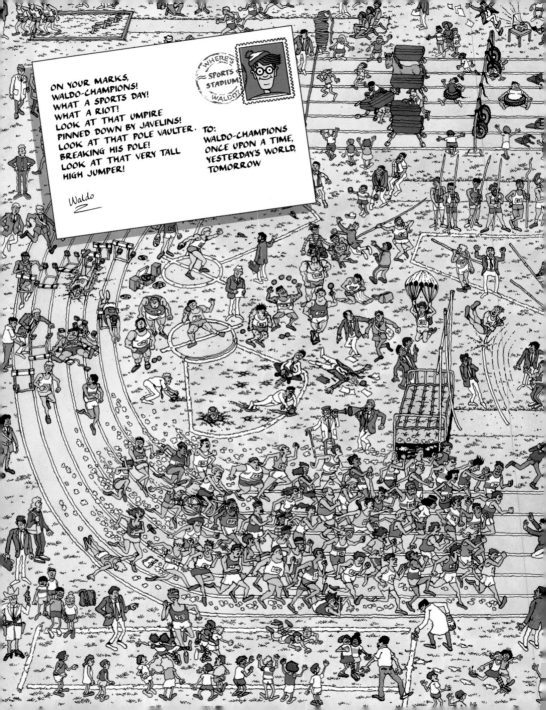

ON YOUR MARKS,
WALDO-CHAMPIONS!
WHAT A SPORTS DAY!
WHAT A RIOT!
LOOK AT THAT UMPIRE
PINNED DOWN BY JAVELINS!
LOOK AT THAT POLE VAULTER.
BREAKING HIS POLE!
LOOK AT THAT VERY TALL
HIGH JUMPER!

Waldo

TO:
WALDO-CHAMPIONS
ONCE UPON A TIME,
YESTERDAY'S WORLD,
TOMORROW

WHERE'S SPORTS STADIUM WALDO

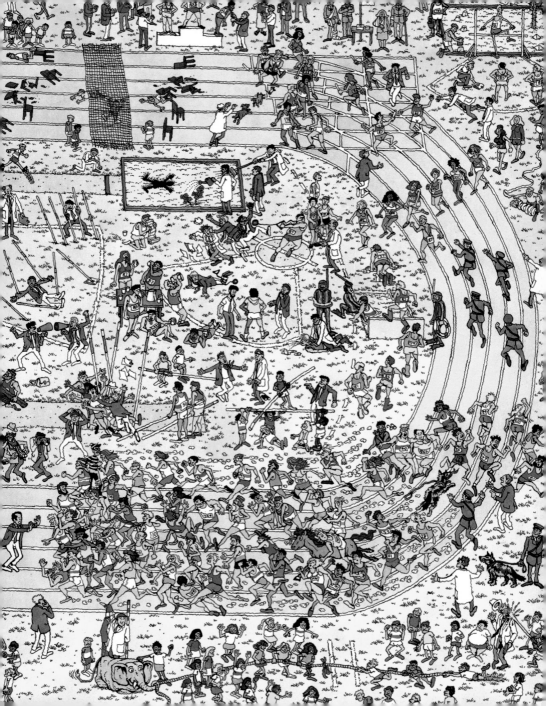

HOW-DE-DOO, WALDO-SCHOLARS!
I'M SMART, AS YOU KNOW.
I GO TO MUSEUMS TO LEARN
THINGS. TODAY I FOUND OUT
ABOUT TICKLING THE TOES OF
A MAN IN THE STOCKS; ABOUT
KNOCKING DOWN A SUIT OF
ARMOR; ABOUT THE
EGYPTIAN MUMMY'S BABY.
NOW, THAT'S LEARNING!

Waldo

TO:
WALDO-SCHOLARS
AT SCHOOL,
IN TROUBLE,
AGAIN

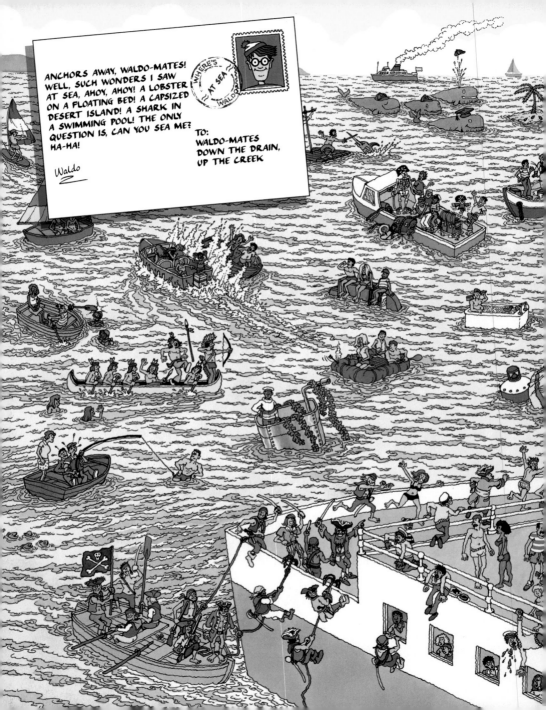

ANCHORS AWAY, WALDO-MATES!
WELL, SUCH WONDERS I SAW
AT SEA, AHOY, AHOY! A LOBSTER
ON A FLOATING BED! A CAPSIZED
DESERT ISLAND! A SHARK IN
A SWIMMING POOL! THE ONLY
QUESTION IS, CAN YOU SEA ME?
HA-HA!

Waldo

TO:
WALDO-MATES
DOWN THE DRAIN,
UP THE CREEK

WHERE'S
AT SEA
WALDO

THE GREAT WHERE'S WALDO?
CHECKLIST: PART TWO

SPORTS STADIUM

- [ ] Three pairs of feet, sticking out of sand
- [ ] A cowboy starting races
- [ ] Hopeless hurdlers
- [ ] Ten children with fifteen legs
- [ ] A record thrower
- [ ] A shot put juggler
- [ ] An ear trumpet
- [ ] A vaulting horse
- [ ] A runner with two wheels
- [ ] A parachuting vaulter
- [ ] A Scotsman with a pole
- [ ] An elephant pulling a rope
- [ ] People being knocked over by a hammer
- [ ] A gardener
- [ ] Three frogmen
- [ ] A nude runner
- [ ] A bed
- [ ] A bandaged boy
- [ ] A runner with four legs
- [ ] A sunken jumper
- [ ] A man with an odd pair of legs
- [ ] A man chasing a dog chasing a cat
- [ ] A boy squirting water

MUSEUM

- [ ] A very big skeleton
- [ ] A clown squirting water
- [ ] A catapult firing a child
- [ ] A bird's nest in a woman's hair
- [ ] A highwayman
- [ ] A popping bicep
- [ ] An arrow in the neck
- [ ] A knight watching TV
- [ ] Picture robbers
- [ ] A smoking picture
- [ ] A leaking watercolor
- [ ] Fighting pictures
- [ ] A king and queen
- [ ] A fat picture and a thin one
- [ ] Three cavemen
- [ ] A game of catch with a bomb
- [ ] Charioteers
- [ ] A collapsing pillar

AT SEA

- [ ] A windsurfer
- [ ] A boat punctured by an arrow
- [ ] A sword fight with a swordfish
- [ ] A school of whales
- [ ] Seasick sailors
- [ ] A leaking diver
- [ ] A boat crash
- [ ] A bathtub
- [ ] A seabed
- [ ] A game of tic-tac-toe
- [ ] A lucky fisherman
- [ ] Three lumberjacks
- [ ] Unlucky fishermen
- [ ] Two water-skiers in a tangle
- [ ] Fish robbers
- [ ] A sea cowboy
- [ ] A fishy photo
- [ ] A man being strangled by an octopus
- [ ] Stowaways
- [ ] A Chinese junk
- [ ] A wave at sea

SAFARI PARK

- [ ] Noah's ark
- [ ] A message in a bottle
- [ ] A hippo having its teeth cleaned
- [ ] A bird's nest in an antler
- [ ] A hungry giraffe
- [ ] An ice cream robber
- [ ] A zebra crossing
- [ ] Santa Claus
- [ ] Three owls
- [ ] A unicorn
- [ ] Caged people
- [ ] A lion driving a car
- [ ] Bears
- [ ] Tarzan
- [ ] Lion cubs
- [ ] An Indian tiger
- [ ] Two lines for the restrooms
- [ ] Animals' beauty parlor
- [ ] An elephant squirting water

DEPARTMENT STORE

- [ ] An ironing demonstration
- [ ] A woman surprised undressing
- [ ] A man whose boots face the wrong way
- [ ] A man with heavy packages
- [ ] A misbehaving vacuum cleaner
- [ ] Ties that match their wearers
- [ ] A man washing his clothes
- [ ] A man trying on a jacket that's too big
- [ ] A woman tripping over toys
- [ ] A boy pulling a girl's hair
- [ ] A boy riding in a shopping cart
- [ ] A glove that's alive

FAIRGROUND

- [ ] A cannon at a rifle range
- [ ] A bumper car run wild
- [ ] A sword swallower
- [ ] A one-armed bandit
- [ ] A helium-balloon seller
- [ ] A runaway rocket
- [ ] A runaway merry-go-round horse
- [ ] A haunted house
- [ ] Seven lost children and a lost dog
- [ ] A tank crash
- [ ] A weight lifter dropping his weights
- [ ] Three clowns
- [ ] Three men dressed as bears

WOW! WHAT A SEARCH!

Did you find Waldo, all his friends, and all the things they lost? Did you find the one scene where Waldo and Odlaw both lost their binoculars? Odlaw's binoculars are the ones nearest to him. Did you find the extra character who appears in every scene? If not, keep looking! Wow! Fantastic!

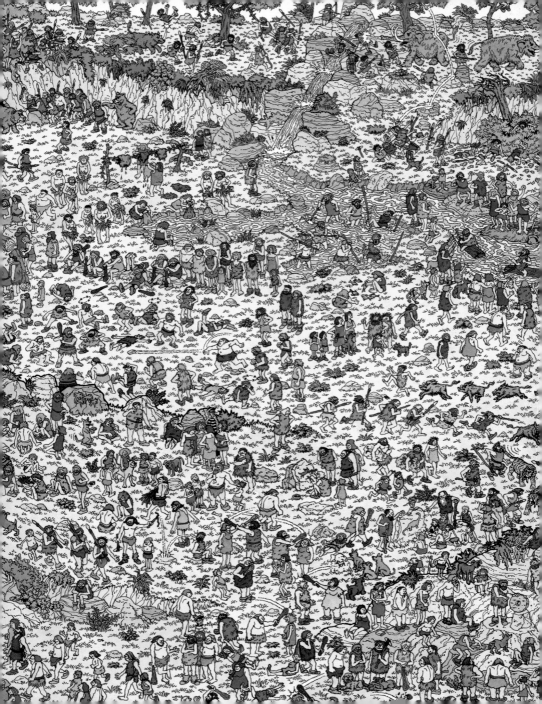

4,578 YEARS AGO

THE RIDDLE OF THE PYRAMIDS

THE ANCIENT EGYPTIANS WERE VERY CLEVER PEOPLE WHO LIVED GOATS, CATS AND SPHINX, AND WHO INVENTED PYRAMIDS. THEY BUILT SEVERAL HUGE PYRAMIDS IN THE DESERT. BUT NOW NO ONE CAN REMEMBER WHY. WERE THEY ADVENTURE PLAYGROUNDS FOR EGYPTIAN MUMMIES AND BABIES, OR WERE THEY HOUSES WITHOUT DOORS OR WINDOWS? TO ANSWER THOSE QUESTIONS AND TO FIND ME CAN BE AS HARD AS A CAMEL'S HUMP.

2,000 YEARS AGO

FVN AND GAMES IN ANCIENT ROME

THE ROMANS SPENT MOST OF THEIR TIME FIGHTING, CONQVERING, LEARNING LATIN AND MAKING ROADS. THEY ALWAYS HAD GAMES AT THE COLISEVM. THEIR FAVORITE GAMES WERE FIGHTING, CHARIOT RACING, FIGHTING, AND FEEDING CHRISTIANS TO THE LIONS. WHEN THE CROWD GAVE A GLADIATOR THE THVMBS DOWN, IT MEANT KILL YOVR OPPONENT. THVMBS VP MEANT LET HIM GO. THVMBS VP FOR YOV IF YOV CAN FIND ME AT THE GAMES.

800 YEARS AGO

The End of the Crusades

After 200 years of fierce argument with the Saladins and Paladins, who would not tell them the way to Jerusalem, the Crusaders finally ran out of clean T-shirts, so they came home. For years afterward they dined out on stories of the castles they had battered and besieged and the fascinating people they had thrown rocks at. Go on your own crusade to find me.

600 YEARS AGO

ONCE UPON A SATURDAY MORNING

The Middle Ages were a very merry time to be alive, especially on Saturdays. Short skirts and striped tights were in fashion for men; everybody knew lots of jokes; there was widespread juggling, jousting, archery, jesting and fun. But if you got into trouble, the Middle Ages could be miserable. For the man in the stocks or the pillory or about to lose his head, Saturday morning was no laughing matter. Don't joke around, look for me here.

171,185 DAYS AGO

THE LAST DAYS OF THE AZTECS

The Aztecs lived in sunny Mexico and were rich and strong and liked swinging from poles pretending to be eagles. They also liked making human sacrifices to their gods, so it was best to agree with everything they said. The Spanish were also rich and strong and some of them, called conquistadores, came to Mexico to find gold. They thought

the Aztecs a complete nuisance. Get swinging and find me in Mexico.

400 YEARS AGO

Is red better than blue? What do you mean your poem about cherry blossoms is better than mine? Shall we have another cup of tea? Over difficult questions such as these, the Japanese fought fiercely for hundreds of years. The fiercest fighters of all were the samurai, who wore flags on their backs so that their mommies could find them. The fighters without flags were called ashigaru. I don't have a flag either, but find me anyway.

TROUBLE IN OLD JAPAN

BEING A PIRATE
(Shiver-me-timbers!)

It really was a lot of fun being a pirate, especially if you were very hairy and didn't have much in the way of brains. It also helped if you had only one leg, or one eye, or two noses, and had a pirate's hat with your name tag sewn inside and a treasure map and a rusty cutlass. Once there were lots of pirates, but they died out in the end because too many of them were men. Shiver me timbers and find me here.

HAVING A BALL IN GAYE PAREE

The history of France has some very bad parts, like getting your head chopped off by Madame Guillotine in the French Revolution; and some very good parts, like the invention of smelly cheese. In 1870 Napoleon (the third one) threw a ball in Paris to celebrate. All the beautiful people came and danced the night away to a band called the Third Republic. Waltz right in and find me.

100 YEARS AGO

THE GOLD RUSH

At the end of the nineteenth century large numbers of AMERICANS were frequently seen to be RUSHING toward HOLES in the ground, hoping to find GOLD. Most of them never even found the holes in the ground. But at least they all got EXERCISE and FRESH AIR, which kept them HEALTHY. And health is more important than GOLD . . . isn't it? You get the GOLD if you can spot me.

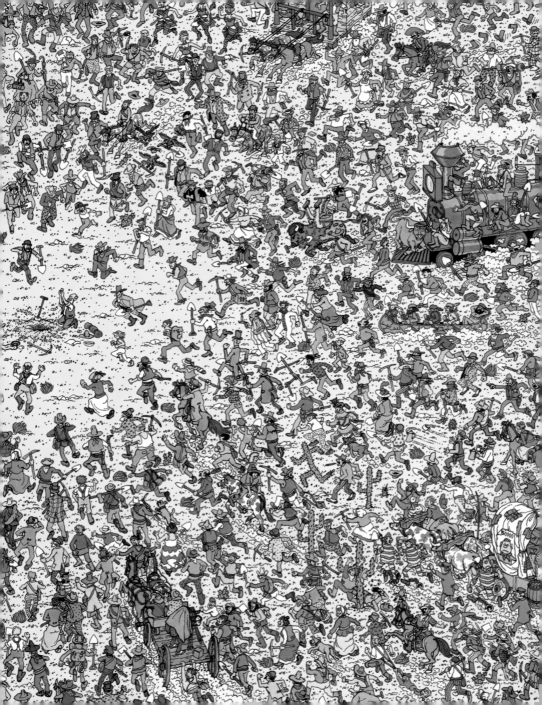

THE GOBBLING GLUTTONS

ONCE UPON A TIME, WALDO
EMBARKED UPON A FANTASTIC
JOURNEY. FIRST, AMONG A
THRONG OF GOBBLING GLUTTONS,
HE MET WIZARD WHITEBEARD, WHO
COMMANDED HIM TO FIND A SCROLL AND
THEN TO FIND ANOTHER AT EVERY STAGE OF
HIS JOURNEY. FOR WHEN HE HAD FOUND
12 SCROLLS, HE WOULD UNDERSTAND THE
TRUTH ABOUT HIMSELF.

IN EVERY PICTURE FIND WALDO, WOOF (BUT
ALL YOU CAN SEE IS HIS TAIL), WENDA, WIZARD
WHITEBEARD, ODLAW, AND THE SCROLL. THEN
FIND WALDO'S KEY, WOOF'S BONE (IN THIS SCENE
IT'S THE BONE THAT'S NEAREST TO HIS TAIL),
WENDA'S CAMERA, AND ODLAW'S BINOCULARS.

THERE ARE ALSO 25 WALDO-WATCHERS, EACH OF
WHOM APPEARS ONLY ONCE SOMEWHERE IN
THE FOLLOWING 12 PICTURES. AND ONE MORE
THING! CAN YOU FIND ANOTHER CHARACTER,
NOT SHOWN BELOW, WHO APPEARS ONCE IN
EVERY PICTURE EXCEPT THE LAST?

WHERE'S
WALDO?
THE
FANTASTIC
JOURNEY

THE GOBBLING GLUTTONS

- [ ] A strong waiter and a weak one
- [ ] Long-distance smells
- [ ] Unequal portions of pie
- [ ] A man who has had too much to drink
- [ ] People who are going the wrong way
- [ ] Very tough dishes
- [ ] An upside-down dish
- [ ] A very hot dinner
- [ ] Knights drinking through straws
- [ ] A clever drink pourer
- [ ] Giant sausages
- [ ] A custard fight
- [ ] An overloaded seat
- [ ] Beard-flavored soup
- [ ] Men pulling legs
- [ ] A painful spillage
- [ ] A poke in the eye
- [ ] A man tied up in spaghetti
- [ ] A knockout dish
- [ ] A man who has eaten too much
- [ ] A tall diner eating a tall dish
- [ ] An exploding pie
- [ ] A giant sausage breaking in half
- [ ] A smell traveling through two people

THE BATTLING MONKS

- [ ] Two fire engines
- [ ] Hotfooted monks
- [ ] A bridge made of monks
- [ ] A smart-alecky monk
- [ ] A diving monk
- [ ] A scared statue
- [ ] Fire meeting water
- [ ] A snaking jet of water
- [ ] Chasers being chased
- [ ] A smug statue
- [ ] A snaking jet of flame
- [ ] A five-way washout
- [ ] A burning bridge
- [ ] Seven burning backsides
- [ ] Monks worshipping the Flowing Bucket of Water
- [ ] Monks shielding themselves from lava
- [ ] Thirteen trapped and extremely worried monks
- [ ] A monk seeing an oncoming jet of flame
- [ ] Monks worshipping the Mighty Erupting Volcano
- [ ] A very worried monk confronted by two opponents
- [ ] A burning hose
- [ ] Monks and lava pouring out of a volcano
- [ ] A chain of water
- [ ] Two monks accidentally attacking their brothers

THE CARPET FLYERS

- [ ] Two carpets on a collison course
- [ ] An overweight flyer
- [ ] A pedestrian crossing
- [ ] A carpet pinup
- [ ] Three hangers-on
- [ ] Flying hitchhikers
- [ ] An unsatisfied customer
- [ ] A used-carpet salesman
- [ ] A topsy-turvy tower
- [ ] A spiky crash
- [ ] Carpet cops and robbers
- [ ] A passing fruit thief
- [ ] Upside-down flyers
- [ ] A carpet repair shop
- [ ] Popular male and female flyers
- [ ] A flying tower
- [ ] A stair carpet
- [ ] Flying highwaymen
- [ ] Rich and poor flyers
- [ ] A carpet-breakdown rescue service
- [ ] Carpets flying on carpet flyers
- [ ] A carpet traffic policeman
- [ ] A flying carpet without a flyer

THE GREAT BALLGAME PLAYERS

- [ ] A three-way drink
- [ ] A row of handheld banners
- [ ] A chase that goes around in circles
- [ ] A spectator surrounded by three rival supporters
- [ ] Players who can't see where they are going
- [ ] Two tall players versus short ones
- [ ] Seven awful singers
- [ ] A face made of balls
- [ ] Players who are digging for victory
- [ ] A face about to hit a fist
- [ ] A shot that breaks the woodwork
- [ ] A mob chasing a player backward
- [ ] A player chasing a mob
- [ ] Players pulling one another's hoods
- [ ] A flag with a hole in it
- [ ] A mob of players all holding balls
- [ ] A player heading a ball
- [ ] A player tripping over a rock
- [ ] A player punching a ball
- [ ] A spectator accidentally hitting two others
- [ ] A player sticking his tongue out at a mob
- [ ] A mouth pulled open by a beard
- [ ] A backside shot

THE FEROCIOUS RED DWARFS

- [ ] A spear-breaking slingshot
- [ ] Two punches causing chain reactions
- [ ] Fat and thin spears and spearmen
- [ ] A spearman being knocked through a flag
- [ ] A collar made out of a shield
- [ ] A prison made of spears
- [ ] Tangled spears
- [ ] A devious disarmer
- [ ] Dwarfs disguised as spearmen
- [ ] A stickup machine
- [ ] A spearman trapped by his battle dress
- [ ] A sneaky spear bender
- [ ] An ax head causing headaches
- [ ] A dwarf who is on the wrong side
- [ ] Prankish target practice
- [ ] Opponents charging through each other
- [ ] A spearman running away from a spear
- [ ] A slingshot causing a chain reaction
- [ ] A sword cutting through a shield
- [ ] A dwarf hiding up a spear
- [ ] Spearmen who have jumped out of their clothes
- [ ] A spear knocking off a dwarf's helmet

THE NASTY NASTIES

- [ ] A vampire who is scared of ghosts
- [ ] Two vampire bears
- [ ] Vampires drinking through straws
- [ ] Gargoyle lovers
- [ ] An upside-down torture
- [ ] A baseball bat
- [ ] Three wolfmen
- [ ] A mummy who is coming undone
- [ ] A vampire mirror test
- [ ] A frightened skeleton
- [ ] Dog, cat, and mouse doorways
- [ ] Courting cats
- [ ] A ghoulish bowling game
- [ ] A gargoyle being poked in the eye
- [ ] An upside-down gargoyle
- [ ] Ghoulish flight controllers
- [ ] Three witches flying backward
- [ ] A witch losing her broomstick
- [ ] A broomstick flying a witch
- [ ] A ticklish torture
- [ ] A vampire about to get the chop
- [ ] A ghost train
- [ ] A vampire who doesn't fit his coffin
- [ ] A three-eyed, hooded torturer

THE GOBBLING GLUTTONS

ONCE UPON A TIME, WALDO
EMBARKED UPON A FANTASTIC
JOURNEY. FIRST, AMONG A
THRONG OF GOBBLING GLUTTONS,
HE MET WIZARD WHITEBEARD, WHO
COMMANDED HIM TO FIND A SCROLL AND
THEN TO FIND ANOTHER AT EVERY STAGE OF
HIS JOURNEY. FOR WHEN HE HAD FOUND
12 SCROLLS, HE WOULD UNDERSTAND THE
TRUTH ABOUT HIMSELF.

IN EVERY PICTURE FIND WALDO, WOOF (BUT
ALL YOU CAN SEE IS HIS TAIL), WENDA, WIZARD
WHITEBEARD, ODLAW, AND THE SCROLL. THEN
FIND WALDO'S KEY, WOOF'S BONE (IN THIS SCENE
IT'S THE BONE THAT'S NEAREST TO HIS TAIL),
WENDA'S CAMERA, AND ODLAW'S BINOCULARS.

THERE ARE ALSO 25 WALDO-WATCHERS, EACH OF
WHOM APPEARS ONLY ONCE SOMEWHERE IN
THE FOLLOWING 12 PICTURES. AND ONE MORE
THING! CAN YOU FIND ANOTHER CHARACTER,
NOT SHOWN BELOW, WHO APPEARS ONCE IN
EVERY PICTURE EXCEPT THE LAST?

THE BATTLING MONKS

THEN WALDO AND WIZARD WHITEBEARD CAME TO THE PLACE WHERE THE INVISIBLE MONKS OF FIRE FOUGHT THE MONKS OF WATER. AND AS WALDO SEARCHED FOR THE SECOND SCROLL, HE SAW THAT MANY WALDOS HAD BEEN THIS WAY BEFORE. AND WHEN HE FOUND THE SCROLL, IT WAS TIME TO CONTINUE WITH HIS JOURNEY.

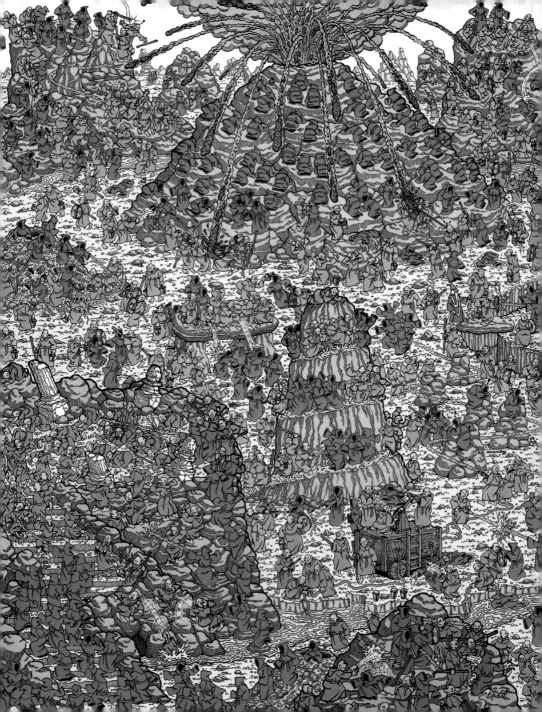

THE CARPET FLYERS

THEN WALDO AND WIZARD WHITEBEARD
CAME TO THE LAND OF THE CARPET FLYERS,
WHERE MANY WALDOS HAD BEEN BEFORE.
AND WALDO SAW THAT THERE WERE MANY
CARPETS IN THE SKY AND MANY RED BIRDS
(HOW MANY, O BRAINY BIRD AND CARPET WATCHERS?).
AND WHEN WALDO FOUND THE THIRD SCROLL, IT WAS
TIME TO CONTINUE WITH HIS JOURNEY.

THE GREAT BALLGAME PLAYERS

THEN WALDO AND WIZARD WHITEBEARD CAME TO THE PLAYING FIELD OF THE GREAT BALLGAME PLAYERS, WHERE MANY WALDOS HAD BEEN BEFORE. AND WALDO SAW THAT FOUR TEAMS WERE PLAYING AGAINST ONE ANOTHER (BUT WAS ANYONE WINNING? WHAT WAS THE SCORE? CAN YOU FIGURE OUT THE RULES?). THEN WALDO FOUND THE FOURTH SCROLL AND CONTINUED WITH HIS JOURNEY.

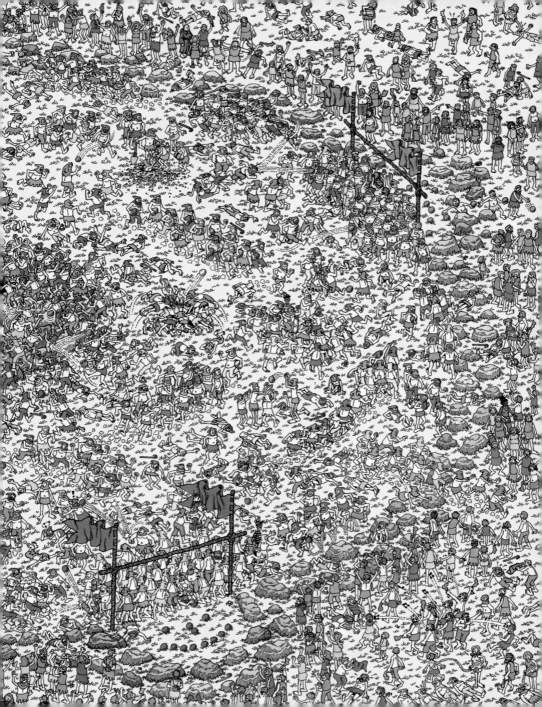

THE FEROCIOUS RED DWARFS

THEN WALDO AND WIZARD WHITEBEARD CAME AMONG THE FEROCIOUS RED DWARFS, WHERE MANY WALDOS HAD BEEN BEFORE. AND THE DWARFS WERE ATTACKING THE MANY-COLORED SPEARMEN, CAUSING MIGHTY MAYHEM AND HORRID HAVOC. AND WALDO FOUND THE FIFTH SCROLL AND CONTINUED WITH HIS JOURNEY.

THE NASTY NASTIES

THEN WALDO AND WIZARD WHITEBEARD CAME TO
THE CASTLE OF THE NASTY NASTIES, WHERE
MANY WALDOS HAD BEEN BEFORE. AND
WHEREVER WALDO WALKED, THERE WAS A FEARFUL CLATTERING
OF BONES (WOOF'S BONE IN THIS SCENE IS THE ONE NEAREST TO
HIS TAIL) AND A FOUL SLURPING OF FILTHY FOOD. AND WALDO
FOUND THE SIXTH SCROLL AND CONTINUED WITH HIS JOURNEY.

THE FIGHTING FORESTERS

THEN WALDO AND WIZARD WHITEBEARD CAME
AMONG THE FIGHTING FORESTERS, WHERE
MANY WALDOS HAD BEEN BEFORE. AND IN
THEIR BATTLE WITH THE EVIL BLACK KNIGHTS,
THE FOREST WOMEN WERE AIDED BY THE ANIMALS, BY
THE LIVING MUD, EVEN BY THE TREES THEMSELVES. AND
WALDO FOUND THE SEVENTH SCROLL AND CONTINUED
WITH HIS JOURNEY.

THE DEEP-SEA DIVERS

THEN WALDO AND WIZARD WHITEBEARD CAME
TO THE WATERY WORLD OF THE DEEP-SEA
DIVERS, WHERE MANY WALDOS HAD BEEN
BEFORE. AND WALDO SEARCHED FOR THE EIGHTH
SCROLL AMONG THE MONSTERS OF THE DEEP, AMONG THE
MERMAIDS, FISHERMEN, AND FISH. AND WHEN HE FOUND IT,
IT WAS TIME TO CONTINUE WITH HIS JOURNEY.

THE KNIGHTS OF THE MAGIC FLAG

THEN WALDO AND WIZARD WHITEBEARD CAME
TO A PLACE MORE CROWDED THAN ANY WALDO
HAD SEEN BEFORE, WHERE TWO ARMIES WITH
MANY MAGIC FLAGS WERE LOCKED IN COMBAT.
AND WALDO SAW THAT MANY WALDOS HAD BEEN THIS WAY
BEFORE. AND WHEN HE FOUND THE NINTH SCROLL, IT WAS
TIME TO CONTINUE WITH HIS JOURNEY.

THE UNFRIENDLY GIANTS

THEN WALDO AND WIZARD WHITEBEARD CAME TO THE LAND OF THE UNFRIENDLY GIANTS, WHERE MANY WALDOS HAD BEEN BEFORE. AND WALDO SAW THAT THE GIANTS WERE HORRIDLY HARASSING THE LITTLE PEOPLE. AND WHEN HE FOUND THE TENTH SCROLL, IT WAS TIME TO CONTINUE WITH HIS JOURNEY.

THE UNDERGROUND HUNTERS

THEN WALDO AND WIZARD WHITEBEARD CAME AMONG THE UNDERGROUND HUNTERS, WHERE MANY WALDOS HAD BEEN BEFORE. THERE WAS MUCH MENACE IN THIS PLACE, AND A MULTITUDE OF MALEVOLENT MONSTERS. WALDO FOUND THE ELEVENTH SCROLL AND CONTINUED WITH HIS JOURNEY.

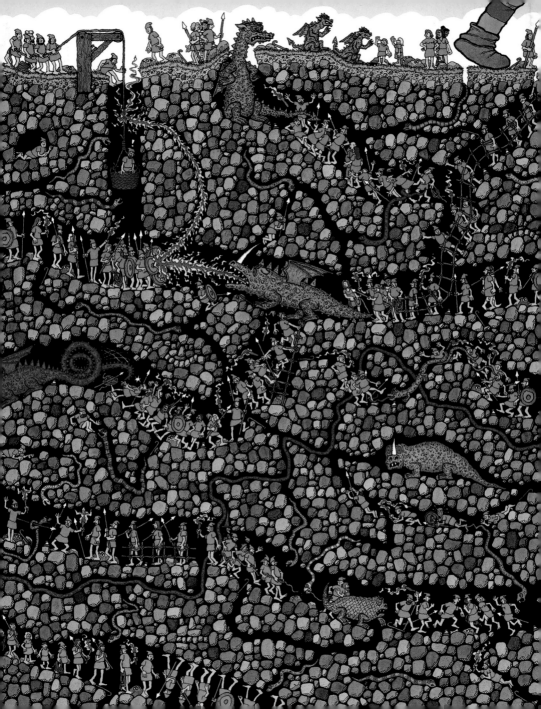

THE LAND OF WALDOS

THEN WALDO FOUND THE TWELFTH SCROLL AND SAW THE
TRUTH ABOUT HIMSELF, THAT HE WAS JUST ONE WALDO
AMONG MANY. HE SAW, TOO, THAT WALDOS OFTEN LOSE
THINGS, FOR HE HIMSELF HAD LOST ONE SHOE. AND AS
HE LOOKED FOR HIS SHOE, HE DISCOVERED THAT WIZARD
WHITEBEARD WAS NOT HIS ONLY FELLOW TRAVELER. THERE WERE NOW
ELEVEN OTHERS—ONE FROM EVERY PLACE HE HAD BEEN TO—
WHO HAD JOINED HIM ONE BY ONE ALONG THE WAY. SO NOW (O LOYAL
FOLLOWERS OF WALDO!) FIND THE REAL WALDO AND HELP HIM FIND HIS
MISSING SHOE. AND THERE, IN THE LAND OF WALDOS,
MAY WALDO LIVE HAPPILY EVER AFTER.

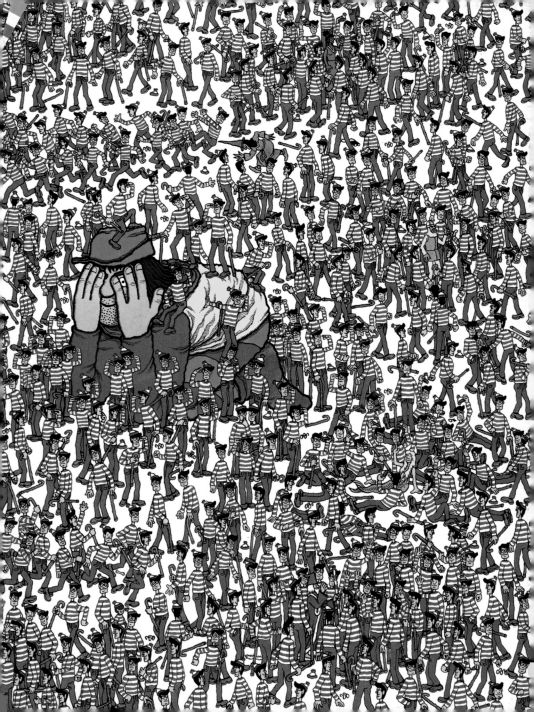

WHERE'S
WALDO?
IN
HOLLYWOOD

A DREAM COME TRUE

WOW, WALDO-WATCHERS, THIS IS FANTASTIC, I'M REALLY IN HOLLYWOOD! LOOK AT THE FILM PEOPLE EVERYWHERE — I WONDER WHAT MOVIES THEY'RE MAKING. THIS IS MY DREAM COME TRUE . . . TO MEET THE DIRECTORS AND ACTORS, TO WALK THROUGH THE CROWDS OF EXTRAS, TO SEE BEHIND THE SCENES! PHEW, I WONDER IF I'LL APPEAR IN A MOVIE MYSELF!

★ ★ ★ WHAT TO LOOK FOR IN HOLLYWOOD! ★ ★ ★

WELCOME TO TINSELTOWN, WALDO-WATCHERS! THESE ARE THE PEOPLE AND THINGS TO LOOK FOR AS YOU WALK THROUGH THE FILM SETS WITH WALDO.

* FIRST (OF COURSE!) WHERE'S WALDO?
* NEXT FIND WALDO'S CANINE COMPANION, WOOF — REMEMBER, ALL YOU CAN SEE IS HIS TAIL!
* THEN FIND WALDO'S FRIEND WENDA!
* ABRACADABRA! NOW FOCUS IN ON WIZARD WHITEBEARD!
* BOO! HISS! HERE COMES THE BAD GUY, ODLAW!
* NOW SPOT THESE 25 WALDO-WATCHERS, EACH OF WHOM APPEARS ONLY ONCE BEFORE THE FINAL FANTASTIC SCENE!
* WOW! INCREDIBLE! SPOT ONE OTHER CHARACTER WHO APPEARS IN EVERY SCENE EXCEPT THE LAST!

★ ★ KEEP ON SEARCHING! THERE'S MORE TO FIND! ★ ★

ON EVERY SET FIND WALDO'S LOST KEY!
WOOF'S LOST BONE! WENDA'S LOST CAMERA! WIZARD WHITEBEARD'S SCROLL!
ODLAW'S LOST BINOCULARS! AND A MISSING CAN OF FILM!

★ ★ ★ ★ ★ ★ AND MORE AND MORE! ★ ★ ★ ★ ★ ★

EACH OF THE FOUR POSTERS ON THE WALL OVER THERE IS PART OF ONE OF THE FILM SETS WALDO IS ABOUT TO VISIT. ★ FIND OUT WHERE THE POSTERS CAME FROM. ★ THEN SPOT ANY DIFFERENCES BETWEEN THE POSTERS AND THE SETS.

SHHH! THIS IS A SILENT MOVIE

SO THIS IS HOW THE HOLLYWOOD DREAM BEGAN – WITH
SILENT MOVIES MADE IN BLACK AND WHITE. IT LOOKS
CRAZY AND IT MAKES YOU LAUGH. ACTING IN SLAPSTICK
COMEDIES MUST BE REALLY HARD – LOOK HOW MANY
ACCIDENTS ARE HAPPENING. BUT THE GREAT THING
IS THAT NONE OF THE ACTORS EVER GET HURT, HOWEVER
OFTEN THEY FALL FLAT ON THEIR FACES!

HORSEPLAY IN TROY

WHAT A SPECTACULAR SCENE THIS IS, WALDO-WATCHERS! AND WHAT AN EPIC COMMOTION PICTURE! I WONDER WHY THE TROJANS DIDN'T GUESS THE WOODEN HORSE WAS FULL OF GREEKS, AND HOW DID THEY GET IT THROUGH THE GATES OF TROY ANYWAY? I WOULDN'T LIKE TO BE IN THE TROJANS' SANDALS, IF THE COSTUME DEPARTMENT HAD GIVEN THEM ANY, THAT IS!

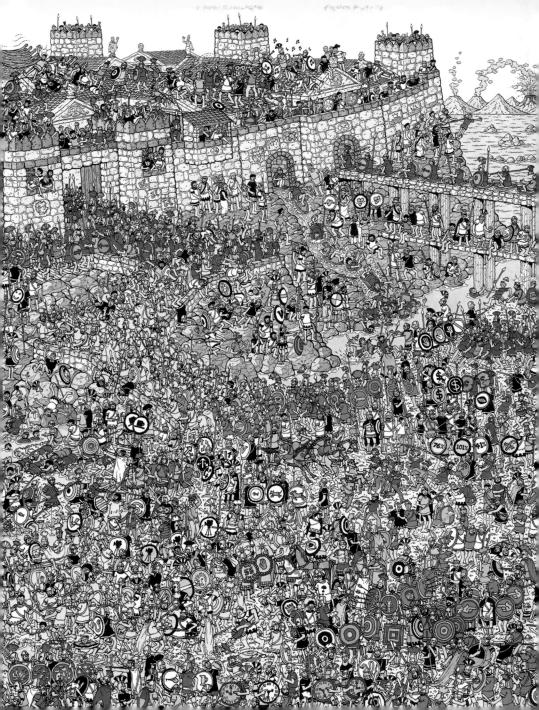

FUN IN THE FOREIGN LEGION

PHEW. MOVIE FANS. DON'T GET OVERHEATED. THIS IS THE MOST SIZZLING LOCATION SO FAR! EVERYONE'S SWELTERING. FROM STARS TO SAND-SHIFTERS. SOME OF THOSE EXTRAS LOOK LIKE THEY'RE LOSING THEIR COOL – HAVE THEY FORGOTTEN THIS IS ONLY A FILM? PERHAPS IT'S TIME A FEW MORE OF THEM DESERTED THE DESERT AND JOINED THE RUSH FOR ICE CREAM!

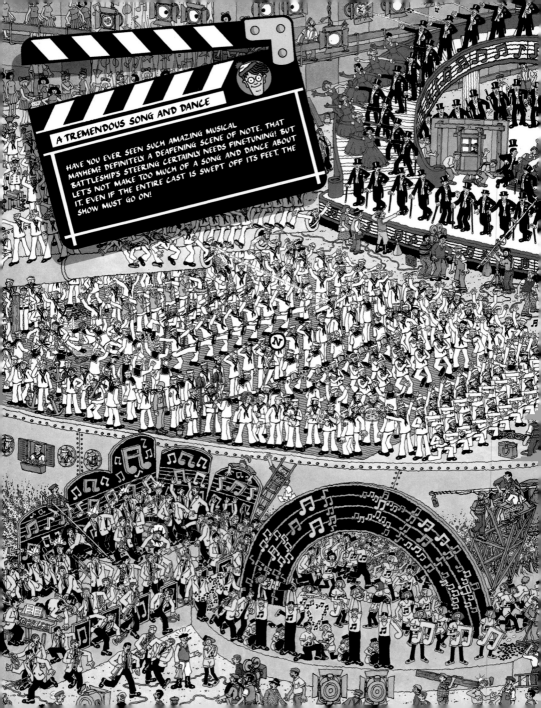

A TREMENDOUS SONG AND DANCE

HAVE YOU EVER SEEN SUCH AMAZING MUSICAL MAYHEM? DEFINITELY A DEAFENING SCENE OF NOTE. THAT BATTLESHIP'S STEERING CERTAINLY NEEDS FINE-TUNING! BUT LET'S NOT MAKE TOO MUCH OF A SONG AND DANCE ABOUT IT. EVEN IF THE ENTIRE CAST IS SWEPT OFF ITS FEET, THE SHOW MUST GO ON!

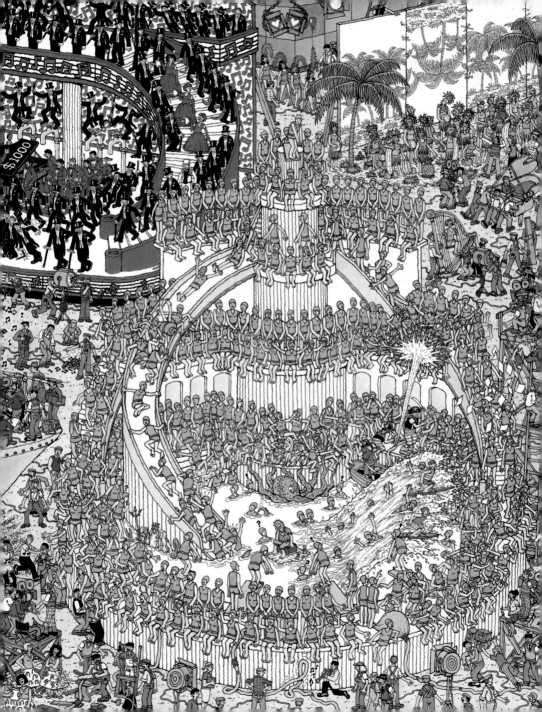

ALI BABA AND THE FORTY THIEVES

WHAT A CRUSH IN THE CAVE, WALDO-FOLLOWERS, BUT PAN IN ON THOSE POTS OF TREASURE! HOW MANY THIEVES WERE IN THE STORY? I BELIEVE THIS DIRECTOR THINKS FORTY THOUSAND! HAVE YOU SPOTTED ALI BABA? HE'S IN THE ALLEY, CUTTING HAIR – THE SCRIPTWRITER THINKS HIS NAME'S ALLEY BARBER! JANGLING GENIES – WHAT A FEARFULLY FUNNY FLICK THIS IS!

THE SWASHBUCKLING MUSKETEERS

ALL FOR ONE, ONE FOR ALL! — WASN'T THAT THE MOTTO OF THE THREE MUSKETEERS? NOW LOOK AT THIS FREE-FOR-ALL! CAN YOU SPOT OUR THREE GALLANT HEROES BATTLING WITH THE RED-COATED CARDINAL'S GUARDS? WITH ALL THIS SWASHBUCKLING ACTION GOING ON, I WONDER HOW THE CAMERAMEN CAN CAPTURE IT ALL ON FILM!

DINOSAURS, SPACEMEN, AND GHOULS

PHEW, INCREDIBLE! TIME, SPACE, AND HORROR ARE IN A MIGHTY MUDDLE HERE! WHAT COSMIC COSTUMES AND WHAT GREAT SPECIAL EFFECTS! ONE OF THOSE FLYING SAUCERS LOOKS LIKE IT'S REALLY FLYING! ARE THOSE REAL ALIENS INSIDE, NOT ACTORS AT ALL? SO WHAT'S REAL AND WHAT'S MADE UP IN FILMS LIKE THESE?

ROBIN HOOD'S MERRY MESS-UP

LOOK HOW MANY MERRY MEN HAVE LEFT SHERWOOD
FOREST FOR A DAY OUT IN NOTTINGHAM CASTLE!
AND WHAT A MERRY TIME THEY'RE HAVING, MESSING
UP THE SHERIFF'S PARADE. WHICH ONE IS ROBIN HOOD? THE
ONE WEARING A ROBIN HOOD, OF COURSE! WHEN
YOU GO TO SEE THIS MOVIE, YOU'LL THINK IT'S ALL REAL,
BUT THE CASTLE'S STONE WALLS ARE MADE OF WOOD!

WOW, WALDO-WATCHERS, THIS IS WHAT I CALL GLAMOUR! I'M AT A MAJOR MOVIE PREMIERE. THE STARS HAVE COME TO SEE THE FILM; THE CROWDS HAVE COME TO SEE THE STARS. LOOK AT THAT PINK STRETCH LIMO – NOW THAT'S A PERFECT CAR FOR A STAR. AND WHO'S IN THE BONE-MOBILE BEHIND? AND DOESN'T KING KONG LOOK NICER IN LIFE THAN WHEN HE'S ON THE SCREEN?

WHERE'S WALDO? THE MUSICAL

WOW, WHAT AN EXTRAVAGANZA, WALDO-WATCHERS – THIS ALL-SINGING, ALL-DANCING MOVIE IS ALL ABOUT ME AND MY FRIENDS! LOOK HOW MANY ACTORS ARE DRESSED UP AS ME! AND LOOK AT ALL THE WOOFS, WENDAS, WIZARD WHITEBEARDS, AND ODLAWS. HAVE YOU NOTICED THAT THE WARDROBE DEPARTMENT HAS MADE MISTAKES WITH SOME OF THE ACTORS' COSTUMES? BUT THAT WON'T HELP YOU FIND THE REAL ME AND MY FOUR FRIENDS IN THIS FILM! I'LL GIVE YOU SOME CLUES. I'M THE WALDO WITH SOMETHING EXTRA FOR WOOF. ALL YOU CAN SEE OF THE REAL WOOF IS HIS TAIL. THE REAL WENDA HAS A CAMERA. THE REAL WIZARD WHITEBEARD IS WEARING A HAT BENT TO THE LEFT. AND THE REAL ODLAW IS HOLDING A WALKING STICK.
THERE'S JUST ONE MORE THING. I'VE BEEN FOLLOWED HERE BY ONE CHARACTER FROM EVERY SET I'VE VISITED. SO CAN YOU SPOT ALL ELEVEN OF THEM IN THIS SCENE? AND CAN YOU FIND OUT WHEN EACH CHARACTER FIRST JOINED ME, AND CATCH ALL THEIR APPEARANCES THROUGHOUT MY TRAVELS?

THE GREAT WHERE'S WALDO? IN HOLLYWOOD CHECKLIST: PART TWO

Even more things for Waldo-Watchers to look for.

★ THE SWASHBUCKLING MUSKETEERS ★

- [ ] Eleven gentlemen bowing
- [ ] Two wheelbarrows
- [ ] Twelve spouts of water
- [ ] A tear-jerking emotional scene
- [ ] A gentleman with only one glove
- [ ] Three musket tears
- [ ] One lost glove
- [ ] A man wearing different colored gloves
- [ ] A hat with a striped plume
- [ ] Badly dressed men turned away from the dance
- [ ] A bouncer
- [ ] Two swordfighting ladies
- [ ] Two dueling film directors
- [ ] Three angry gardeners
- [ ] Two swordsmen fencing
- [ ] Three mixed-up statues
- [ ] A man having his foot tickled
- [ ] Four ladies being presented with flowers
- [ ] Four real animals

★ DINOSAURS, SPACEMEN, AND GHOULS ★

- [ ] "Hand" luggage
- [ ] A fly in saucer
- [ ] A ticklish dinosaur
- [ ] A greedy green alien
- [ ] A dozing dinosaur
- [ ] A spaceship
- [ ] A smart-alecky dinosaur
- [ ] Stars in a star's dressing room
- [ ] A wolfman having a howling good time
- [ ] Eight characters in craters
- [ ] A planet picnic
- [ ] A game of ringtoss
- [ ] A space castle
- [ ] Two people reading books
- [ ] Four cavemen going up in the world
- [ ] An astronaut without helmet, gloves, or boots
- [ ] Three other astronauts without helmets
- [ ] Two bottles of ketchup

★ ROBIN HOOD'S MERRY MESS-UP ★

- [ ] Eight ladies in medieval costume
- [ ] "Little" John leading some men
- [ ] Sixteen flags
- [ ] Two archers with long bows
- [ ] "Maid" Marian cleaning up
- [ ] A medieval extra with a radio
- [ ] A sheriff's soldier with rolled-up sleeves
- [ ] "Fryer" Tuck
- [ ] A night in armor
- [ ] A knight with a pink plume in his helmet
- [ ] The Sheriff of Nottingham
- [ ] A man with a bow and arrow
- [ ] A soldier with a large shield
- [ ] Medieval soldiers wearing the wrong pants
- [ ] A prisoner with a giant ball and chain
- [ ] Five real four-legged animals
- [ ] Twenty-one ladders
- [ ] Seven helmets with animal crests

★ ★ WHEN THE STARS COME OUT ★ ★

- [ ] Twenty-nine lights
- [ ] Two rival news reporters
- [ ] Someone who has it all wrapped up
- [ ] A policeman wanting an autograph
- [ ] Three cowboys
- [ ] Ten hearts
- [ ] Seven large palms
- [ ] Someone with a bird's-eye view
- [ ] A handful of spectators
- [ ] A celebrity wearing a new dress
- [ ] Someone making their mark
- [ ] Two astronauts
- [ ] A sleepy spectator with an alarm clock
- [ ] A twisting telescope
- [ ] An extra-long straw
- [ ] Four celebrities wearing sunglasses

★ ★ WHERE'S WALDO? THE MUSICAL ★ ★

- [ ] A Waldo sweater with stripes in reverse order
- [ ] A Waldo with blond hair
- [ ] A Waldo with a beard
- [ ] A Wenda without any shoes
- [ ] An Odlaw without a mustache
- [ ] A Waldo wearing shades
- [ ] A Waldo sweater with extra stripes
- [ ] A haredresser
- [ ] A Waldo wearing a hat without a bobble
- [ ] A Waldo without pockets on his jeans
- [ ] A Wizard Whitebeard wearing glasses
- [ ] A Waldo script reading
- [ ] A sound mixer
- [ ] A Wenda with a blue-and-white-striped umbrella
- [ ] A walking stick
- [ ] Two Wizard Whitebeards without beards
- [ ] A Waldo without glasses
- [ ] An Odlaw wearing a hat without a bobble
- [ ] A Wenda with blonde hair
- [ ] A Waldo wearing a bobble hat in reverse colors
- [ ] A Wenda without glasses
- [ ] A Wizard Whitebeard wearing a red hat
- [ ] A Woof wearing a bobble hat in reverse colors
- [ ] A Wenda wearing round Waldo glasses
- [ ] A Woof without a bobble hat
- [ ] A Wenda with no pockets on her skirt
- [ ] A Waldo holding a walking stick the wrong way up
- [ ] A Woof wearing a hat without a bobble
- [ ] A Woof wearing shades
- [ ] A back view of a Wenda
- [ ] A Waldo in blue-and-white stripes
- [ ] A Wenda who is not wearing a bobble hat
- [ ] An Odlaw without shades
- [ ] A Wizard Whitebeard dancing
- [ ] A back view of a Waldo
- [ ] A Wizard Whitebeard wearing a bobble hat
- [ ] A Woof wearing a blue-and-white bobble hat
- [ ] Two Wizard Whitebeards without white beards
- [ ] A Wenda wearing a hat without a bobble
- [ ] A Waldo with two bobble hats

★ ★ ★ BACK TO THE BEGINNING ★ ★ ★

Did you find Waldo, all his friends, and all the things they lost? Did you find the mystery character who appears in every scene except the last? And one more thing: Somewhere one of the Waldo-Watchers lost the bobble from his hat. Can you spot which one and find the bobble?

★ ★ ★ THE FINAL FILM TEST ★ ★ ★

Nearly all the faces in the sprocket holes on this and on part one of the checklist appear in color somewhere else in the book. Can you find where? But . . . ten of them do not appear anywhere else! Can you tell which ten? Lastly . . . some faces appear more than once in the sprocket holes. Can you see which ones and how many times each one appears?

THE MIGHTY FRUIT FIGHT

WOW! AMAZING! HAVE YOU EVER IN YOUR LIVES SEEN A PLACE SO FULL OF FRUIT? HOW SWEET IT IS TO SAIL LEMON BOATS DOWN ORANGE JUICE RIVERS! BUT WATCH OUT, WALDO FANS! THE APPLES HAVE TURNED SOUR AND THEY'RE ATTACKING ALL THE OTHER FRUIT. WHOOSH! SQUIRT! SPLOOOOOSH! THERE'S A FRUIT JAM IN THE RIVER, SCUFFLES ON THE BANANA BRIDGES, AND SUGAR BEING POURED ALL OVER THE STRAWBERRIES! PHEW! WHAT A MIGHTY FRUIT FIGHT!

THE GAME OF GAMES

FOUR HUGE TEAMS ARE PLAYING THIS GREAT GAME OF GAMES. THE REFEREES ARE TRYING TO SEE THAT NO ONE BREAKS THE RULES. BETWEEN THE STARTING LINE AT THE TOP AND THE FINISH LINE AT THE BOTTOM, THERE ARE LOTS OF PUZZLES, BOOBY TRAPS, AND TESTS. THE GREEN TEAMS NEARLY WON, AND THE ORANGE TEAMS HARDLY STARTED! CAN YOU SPOT THE ONLY ORANGE TEAM PLAYER WHO HAS FINISHED? AND THE ONLY GREEN TEAM PLAYER WHO HAS NOT YET BEGUN?

BRIGHT LIGHTS AND NIGHT FRIGHTS

HEY! WHAT BLAZING BEAMS OF LIGHT, WHAT A DAZZLING DISPLAY! GLITTER, TWINKLE, SPARKLE, FLASH—LOOK HOW BRIGHTLY THESE LIGHTHOUSES LIGHT UP THE NIGHT! BUT, OH NO, THE MONSTERS WANT TO PUT THE LIGHTS OUT! THEY'RE ATTACKING FROM ALL SIDES. THE SAILORS ARE SQUIRTING PINK GOO AT THEM, BUT THE MONSTERS SPURT GREEN GOO RIGHT BACK! BUT WAIT! THREE OF THE MONSTERS ARE FIRING DIFFERENT COLORED GOO! SPLASH, SPLAT, SPLURGE! CAN YOU SEE THEM, WALDO-WATCHERS?

THE CAKE FACTORY

MMMM! FEAST YOUR EYES, WALDO-WATCHERS! SNIFF THE DELICIOUS SMELLS OF BAKING CAKES! DROOL AT THE TASTY TOPPINGS! CAN YOU SEE A CAKE LIKE A TEAPOT, A CAKE LIKE A HOUSE, A CAKE SO TALL A WORKER ON THE FLOOR ABOVE IS LICKING IT? CAKES, CAKES, EVERYWHERE! HOW SCRUMPTIOUS! HOW YUM-YUM-YUMPTIOUS! LOOK AT THE OOZING SUGAR ICING AND THE SHINY RED CHERRIES ON THE ROOF UP THERE! THAT ROOM IS WHERE THE FACTORY CONTROLLERS WORK, BUT HAVE THEY LOST CONTROL?

THE ODLAW SWAMP

THE BRAVE ARMY OF MANY HATS IS TRYING TO GET THROUGH THIS FEARFUL SWAMP. HUNDREDS OF ODLAWS AND BLACK-AND-YELLOW SWAMP CREATURES ARE CAUSING TROUBLE IN THE UNDERGROWTH. THE REAL ODLAW IS THE ONE CLOSEST TO HIS LOST PAIR OF BINOCULARS. CAN YOU FIND HIM, X-RAY-EYED ONES? HOW MANY

DIFFERENT KINDS OF HATS CAN YOU SEE ON THE SOLDIERS' HEADS? SQUELCH! SQUELCH! I'M GLAD I'M NOT IN THEIR SHOES! ESPECIALLY AS THEIR FEET ARE IN THE MURKY MUD!

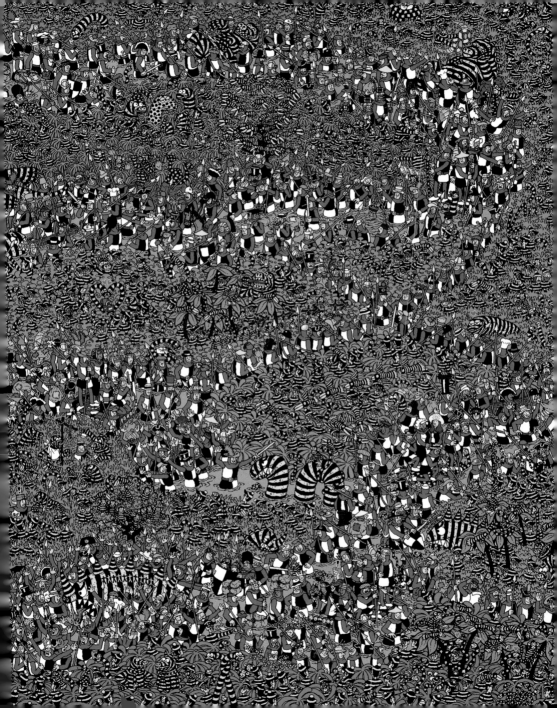

CLOWN TOWN

Clap your feet, Waldo-jokers! Stamp your hands! You'll go oogly-boogly-woogly-eyed with wonder! Here are hundreds of clowns playing pranks and making mischief! Look at their colorful costumes — with fluffy pom-poms galore! And their bright and shiny noses! Toot, toot! Can you see a car with its tongue sticking out?

Ting-a-ling! And a bike with square wheels! Tee-hee! Ha-ha! What happiness it is to be in Clown Town! Splash! Splat! Except for all those squirty flowers and custard pies!

THE FANTASTIC FLOWER GARDEN

CAN YOU SEE? SNIFF THE AIR, WALDO-FOLLOWERS! SMELL THE FANTASTIC SCENTS! WHAT A TREAT FOR YOUR NOSES AS WELL AS YOUR EYES!

WOW! WHAT A BRIGHT AND DAZZLING GARDEN SPECTACLE! ALL THE FLOWERS ARE IN FULL BLOOM, AND HUNDREDS OF BUSY GARDENERS ARE WATERING AND TENDING THEM. THE PETAL COSTUMES THEY ARE WEARING MAKE THEM LOOK LIKE FLOWERS THEMSELVES! VEGETABLES ARE GROWING IN THE GARDEN TOO. HOW MANY DIFFERENT KINDS

THE CORRIDORS OF TIME

TICK-TOCK, TICK-TOCK! THE HANDS OF ALL THE CLOCKS EXCEPT ONE SAY A QUARTER TO TWELVE. WHAT A DING-DONG THERE WILL BE WHEN THEY STRIKE! CAN YOU FIND THE ONLY CLOCK THAT TELLS A DIFFERENT TIME? IN THIS SCENE ARE THIRTY-SEVEN DOORS. ABOVE EACH DOOR APPEARS THE SHAPE OF THE KEY THAT WILL UNLOCK IT. CAN YOU FIND THE KEYS IN THE CROWD, BRAINY ONES, AND MATCH THEM TO THE SHAPES? OH, NO! ONE DOOR HAS NO SHAPE ABOVE IT! EVEN SO, YOU MUST FIND ITS KEY!

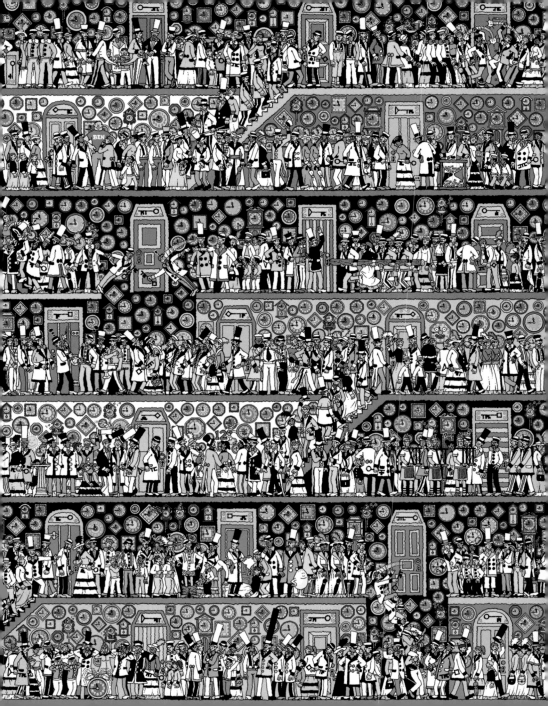